**by Jarrett Mentink, Ph.D.**
**illustrations by Patrick Carlson**

This book is dedicated to those who stand up for people in need.



Printed in China, First Edition.
Published by Kids In The Clouds™
www.kidsintheclouds.com

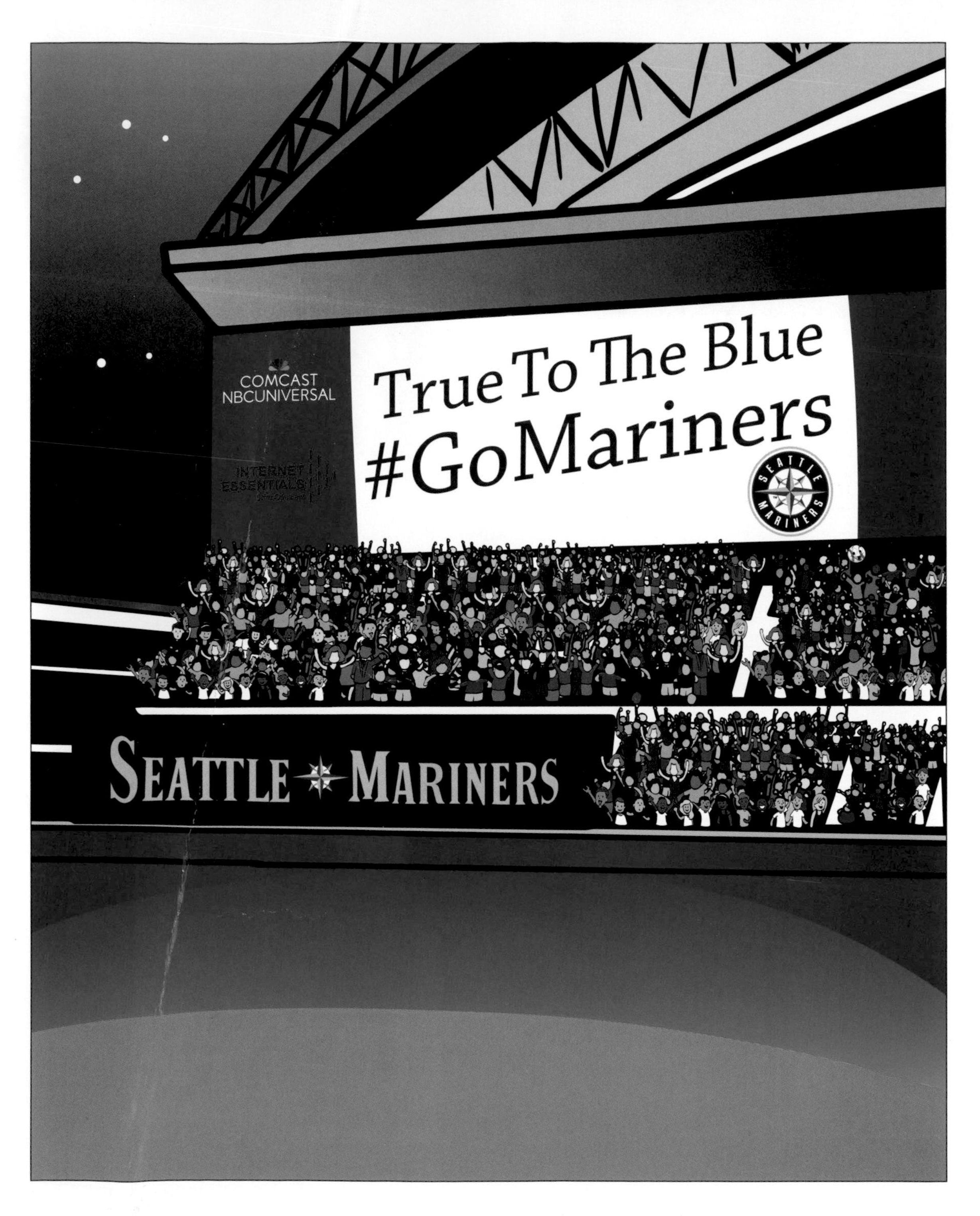


This is a story
of King Felix's steed,
With a cool cyber message
for all fans to read.

His steed as you know
has antlers and fur,
For he is the Moose
that makes Safeco stir.

It was a warm summer night,
Moose was prepping to rock.
He picked up his smartphone
for a check of the clock.

Moose had 20 minutes
to reach the dugout rooftop,
So he paused at his locker
and decided to shop.

He was looking online
for a new **sideburn** kit,
That matched both his eyes
and his Elvis outfit.

Up popped a tweet
that made the Moose frown,
From a colossal mascot
that liked to bring others down!

The Titan's tweet read:
"Moose is a fool.
He wears double zero -
He could not count in school!"

Moose tried to ignore
the Titan's remarks
But felt a deep hurt
from the bullying barks!

As Moose reached the top
of the home dugout step,
It was clear he was missing
his usual pep.

King Felix was pitching
that night at the park.
His sinker was biting
like a razor-toothed shark.

The King was tossing up zeroes
with the help of his knights.
All was well in the Safe
until out went the lights!

The big screen in center
made a loud POP,
Up came a picture
that made Moose's heart drop!

It was a photo of him
as a very young steed,
With tennis balls in his snout
to stop a nosebleed.

The Titan had gained
control of the screen
And was posting the pic
just to be mean!

To the Titan's surprise
the crowd didn't laugh,
For Safeco Field fans
felt bad for the calf.

On top of the mound
in the dark Felix stood,
And did what all friends
in that moment should:

He yelled, "My good Moose,
my trusty steed,
I shall stand by your side
when you are in need!"

But when the lights came back on
his steed wasn't there –
In the dark he had vanished
in the night air!

The big screen bullying
brought the Moose shame.
He'd run from his perch
in the heart of the game.

Felix looked for his friend
and then heard the Moose weep -
hiding by the wood bats
the knights grabbed to go deep!

The King stepped toward Moose,
to comfort his sob,
When out roared the three-wheeler
of Groundskeeper Bob!

The Titan had taken
Bob's speedy land cruiser
To tow a cold-hearted banner
with #MooseLoser.

The knights of King Felix
tried all that they could.

They ran and they dove,
not one of them stood!

But Groundskeeper Bob's
three-wheeler had juice.

The Titan zoomed by the dugout
and laughed at the Moose.

But just as he did
King Felix got set,

And made a pitch for the ages
fans will never forget.

It was right on the mark
to the left of the gas.
The ball hit the brake
and the Titan hit grass!

He tumbled so far,
he ended clear out in left,
No doubt rethinking
his three-wheeling theft!

The King and his mates
raced to the scene.

Felix said, “Titan,
it doesn’t pay to be mean!”

Titan stood up
and gazed at the seats,
Where knights dressed in yellow
ate turkey leg meats.

Together as one,
the entire King's Court
Was showing the Moose
upstanding support!

The Knights were now holding
signs as they stood
But they didn't have "K's"
as they normally would

Instead they spelled out
a message for those,
Who felt picked on for things
like a tennis ball nose.

With his arm on the Moose,
the King pointed above.
Their signs read, “No haters in Safeco
#MooseLove!”

The King tipped his cap
to the Knights of his Court,
"Thank you my friends
for defending our fort!"

"Those that poke fun
at others online
May think that they're cool
but they're no friends of mine!"

King Felix proclaimed,
"Let it be known -
My house of Safeco
is a bully-free zone!"

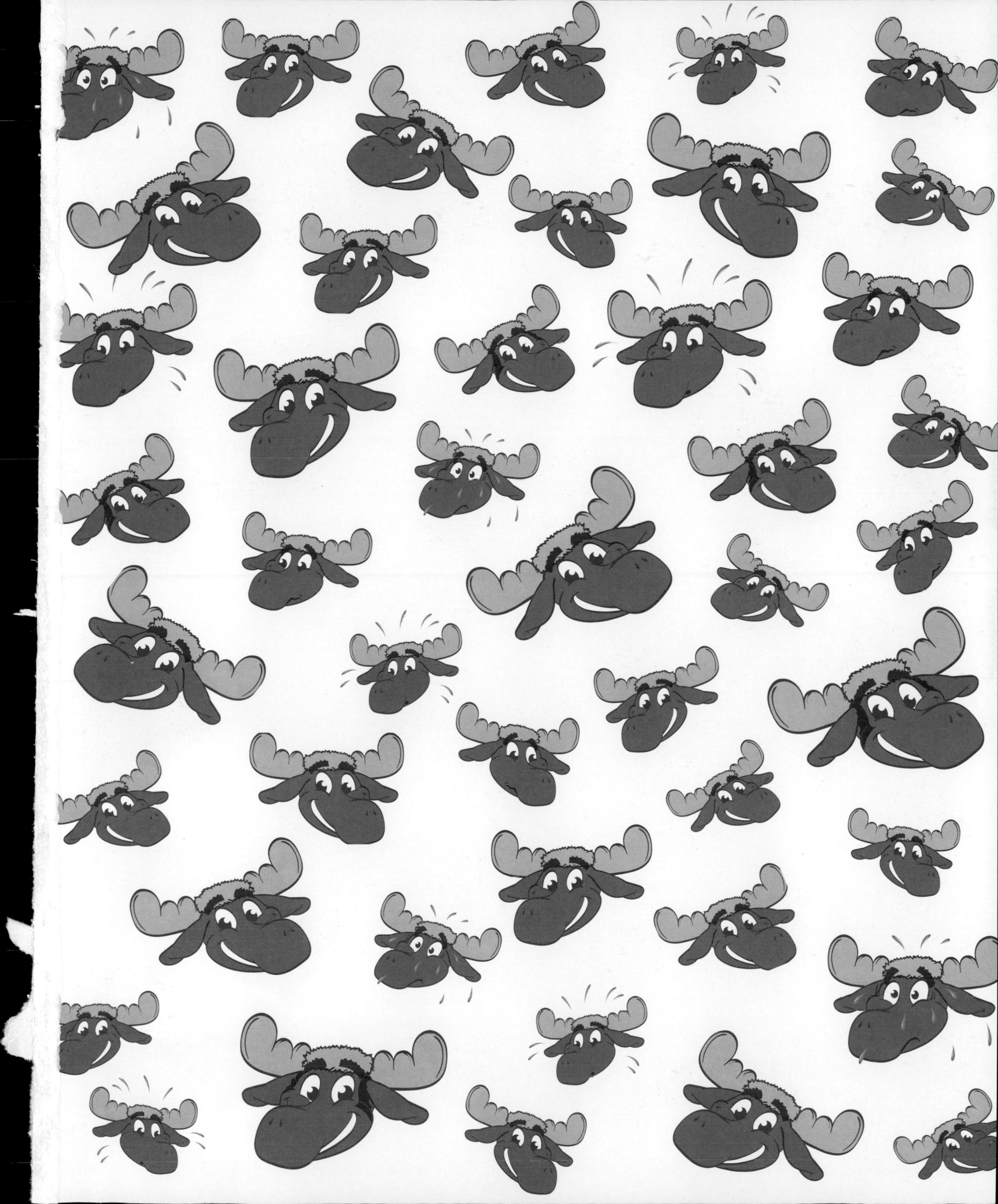